To celebrate the 'Big Birthday Year' of Jo and Brian –
Nana and Grandad – much loved by Hanna, Maddy, Clara,
Abigail, Benjamin and Jake – and by me, of course P.D.E.

For Lily Grace, with love D.A.

First published 2010 by Macmillan Children's Books
This edition published 2014 by Macmillan Children's Books
a division of Macmillan Publishers Limited
20 New Wharf Road, London N1 9RR
Basingstoke and Oxford
Associated companies throughout the world
www.panmacmillan.com

ISBN: 978-1-4472-8222-8

Text copyright © Pamela Duncan Edwards 2010
Illustrations copyright © Deborah Allwright 2010
Moral rights asserted

2 4 6 8 9 7 5 3 1

A CIP catalogue record for this book is available from the British Library.

Printed in China

Dinosaur
Sleepover

Pamela Duncan Edwards

Illustrated by Deborah Allwright

MACMILLAN CHILDREN'S BOOKS

What would you do if it was your cousin's birthday and he invited you and Dinosaur to a sleepover party? What if Dinosaur looked puzzled?

You'd say, "We'll all have fun at the party,
Dinosaur. Then everyone gets to stay overnight."

What if Dinosaur shook his handsome dinosaur head and said in a firm voice, "A dinosaur can't stay overnight because his family would miss him too much."

You'd say, "That's OK, Dinosaur, we can ask Pickles to look after our family while we're gone."

What if Dinosaur tapped his sparkling dinosaur teeth and said in an anxious voice, "Dinosaurs have to brush their teeth before they go to bed. I wouldn't have my toothbrush with me."

You'd say, "That's no problem, Dinosaur. We'll take our things in your stripy washbag and we'll put your toothbrush in the pocket on the side."

What if Dinosaur blinked his bright dinosaur eyes and said in a worried voice, "If a dinosaur did go visiting, he'd have to take clean pyjamas. My pyjamas are in the wash!"

You'd say, "But you've got two pairs of pyjamas, Dinosaur. Your other pair is folded and ready to pack."

What if Dinosaur made himself very small and said in a nervous voice, "I'm afraid they'll forget to come for us in the morning. What if we have to sleep over forever and ever?"

You'd give Dinosaur a huge hug and say, "I tell you what, Dinosaur, we'll write a big note and stick it on the fridge. We'll say . . .

please pick us up
tomorrow at 10.00

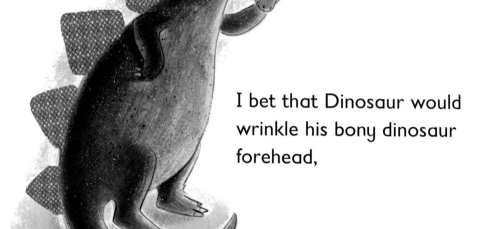

I bet that Dinosaur would wrinkle his bony dinosaur forehead,

and think very hard . . .

Then he'd say, "OK!" And off you'd go.

What if you were walking up the path to the party
and Dinosaur gave a gasp and cried, "I didn't bring
Teddy! A dinosaur can't sleep without his teddy."

You'd laugh and say, "Silly old Dinosaur. You put Teddy in your special bag. His head is poking out of the top." And I bet Dinosaur would laugh, too.

What if you opened the door to the party and everyone said,

"HELLO!"

I bet Dinosaur would smile his huge, toothy
dinosaur smile and run to join the games.

Then you'd all play musical chairs,

and hide-and-seek,

and catch the dinosaur's tail.

And lots of other games, until
the birthday cake arrived.

And after your cousin had blown out all the candles,

I bet Dinosaur would eat a DINO-SIZED
piece of cake!

When it was time for bed, I bet everyone would chatter and giggle

and maybe have a pillow fight.

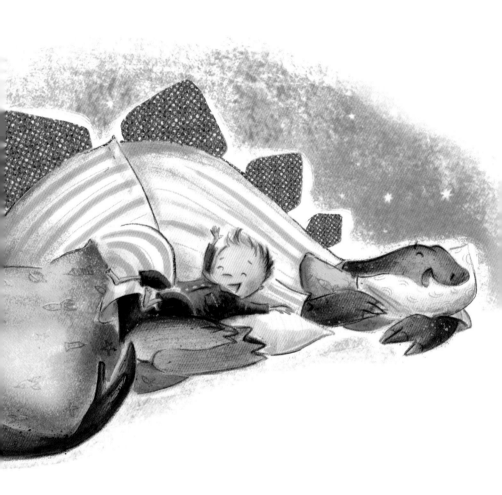

Then you'd laugh and laugh until you were all so
tired you just had to go to sleep.

What if you were snuggled deep down in your sleeping bag and Dinosaur whispered in his happy dinosaur voice, "When it's our birthday, should we have a sleepover party?"

Then I bet you'd say, **"Great idea, Dinosaur!"**